After HAPPILY —EVER— AFTER

Mr. Wolf
Bounces Back

After Happily Ever After is published by Stone Arch Books
A Capstone Imprint
1710 Roe Crest Drive
North Mankato, Minnesota 56003
www.capstonepub.com

First published by Orchard Books, a division of Hachette Children's Books
338 Euston Road, London NW1 3BH, United Kingdom

Library of Congress Cataloging-in-Publication Data is available
on the Library of Congress website.

ISBN-13: 978-1-4342-6414-5

Summary:
Now that the big bad wolf has three cubs of his own, being the
neighborhood bully doesn't seem right. He needs a new job.
Find out if he can find a job that's right for a strong, fast, scary wolf.

Designer:
Russell Griesmer

Photo Credits:
ShutterStock / Maaike Boot, 5, 6, 7, 52, 53, 54, 55

After HAPPILY —EVER— AFTER

Mr. Wolf
Bounces Back

by TONY BRANDMAN

illustrated by SARAH WARBURTON

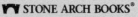
STONE ARCH BOOKS®

a capstone imprint

TABLE OF CONTENTS

Chapter One...............8

Chapter Two...............18

Chapter Three...........23

Chapter Four.............37

Chapter Five.............46

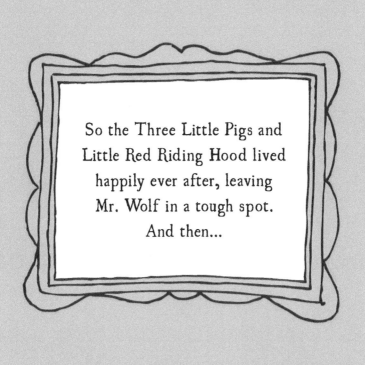

So the Three Little Pigs and
Little Red Riding Hood lived
happily ever after, leaving
Mr. Wolf in a tough spot.
And then...

CHAPTER ONE

Night was falling. Shadows were gathering around Mr. Wolf as he walked down the path toward home.

It had been a very bad day. For one thing, Mr. Wolf had failed to catch any of the Three Little Pigs. He could easily have snapped up the first two. Yet, for some reason, he let them get away.

Though he huffed and puffed at the third little pig's house, his heart hadn't really been in it.

And what a disaster with Little Red Riding Hood! It had all been going so well too. He had enjoyed pretending to be her granny and playing the "what big eyes and teeth you've got" game.

Then suddenly, that nasty woodcutter had
burst into the cottage and chased him with
an axe.

"Oh no!" said Mrs. Wolf when Mr. Wolf got home. "Are you all right, dear? What happened this time?"

"It's a long story," said Mr. Wolf, sitting down. "Actually, it's two long stories, but I'll tell you later. Where are the cubs?"

"Daddy!" squeaked three bundles of gray fur. They raced up to him and jumped onto his lap. He couldn't help smiling, even though he was worn out.

"What's for dinner, Daddy?" they asked.

"I'm sorry, kids," said Mr. Wolf. "I was hoping we'd be having roast pig this evening, but I had a few problems."

"Don't worry," said Mrs. Wolf cheerfully.
"Too much meat probably isn't good for us.
I'll fix something else."

CHAPTER TWO

And that's what she did. The supper she made was very tasty. Afterwards Mr. Wolf played with the cubs.

And at bedtime he read them their favorite stories.

Once they were asleep, he made a
nice pot of tea and sat by the fire with
Mrs. Wolf.

"I used to be so good at bringing home
the bacon," he muttered. "But these days
I'm just hopeless."

He couldn't understand it. He'd always been known in the forest as the Big Bad Wolf. He was the strongest, fastest, and scariest wolf of them all. So why couldn't he catch anything for his family to eat?

Suddenly, he realized what the problem was. He couldn't hurt little creatures anymore. These days they all reminded him of his own cubs.

"That's it," Mr. Wolf said. "I've come to a decision."

"Really?" said Mrs. Wolf. "What are you going to do?"

"I'll get a different job," said Mr. Wolf. "That's what!"

CHAPTER THREE

The next morning, Mr. Wolf rose early
and washed and combed his fur.

He waved goodbye to Mrs. Wolf and
dropped the cubs off at school.

Then he headed for the Forest Job Center.
He took a deep breath and went in.

He sat in the waiting room. Then he was
shown into the office of Mrs. Bear.

"Hello," she said, smiling. "How may
I help you today?"

"I'd like a job," Mr. Wolf said nervously.
"Please."

"Okay, just fill out this form for me,"
said Mrs. Bear. "You don't have many
qualifications, do you? Apart from being
strong, fast, and scary, that is. What kind
of a job did you have in mind?"

"I think I need a complete career change," said Mr. Wolf.

"Terrific!" said Mrs. Bear, peering at her computer. "I like a challenge. Ah, here we are. This one is very different."

Mrs. Bear sent him to the Forest China
Shop, and the manager gave him the job.
But the shop was full of delicate plates,
bowls, and cups.

Mr. Wolf didn't know his own strength,
and he kept breaking things when he picked
them up. He did a lot of damage with his
tail too.

He was back at the Forest Job Center long before lunchtime.

"Don't worry," said Mrs. Bear. "Hmm, now let me see. You enjoy running around in the open air, don't you? Try this one."

The next day, Mr. Wolf went to the Forest Post Office, where they gave him a job delivering the mail.

"This is more like it!" he said.

But he raced through his route so fast that he upset the other carriers. They couldn't compete and said he was a show-off.

Mr. Wolf walked back to Mrs. Bear, his tail tucked between his legs.

"You're turning out to be more of a challenge than I thought," said Mrs. Bear. "But I'm not giving up. Try this one."

So the next morning, Mr. Wolf went to the palace, where he was given a job as a royal servant.

He was more nervous than ever now, but he was determined to do his best. And things didn't go too badly to begin with.

Later that day, there was a royal banquet, and Mr. Wolf was kept very busy. Some of the guests weren't very nice. In fact, the Ugly Sisters and the Wicked Stepmother were so rude that he finally lost his temper.

This time, Mr. Wolf didn't wait to be fired.
He went straight home to his family.

That evening, Mr. Wolf looked down at his little cubs as they lay sleeping. He was really worried now. He wasn't making any money or bringing home any food, and soon the cupboard would be completely bare.

CHAPTER FOUR

At the Forest Job Center the next day,
Mrs. Bear was looking grim.

"Too strong, too fast, too scary," she said.

"I'm sorry, but I give up," she said. "I can't find you a job. Why don't you go back to what you used to do? Now if you don't mind, I've got another appointment."

Mr. Wolf left her office and stood in the shadows of the hallway. He was so miserable he barely noticed the couple going into Mrs. Bear's office.

Then he heard something through the door that caught his attention, and he crept over to listen.

"We're really worried about our little
ones," somebody was saying.

"I'm really worried about mine too,"
thought Mr. Wolf. He sneaked a peek
around the door, and saw that it was
Mr. Pig talking.

"We still think of them as little even though
they have left home," said Mr. Pig.

"Last week was awful," said Mrs. Pig.
"It made us think it might be a good idea
to hire somebody to keep an eye on them."

"Like a sort of security guard?" asked
Mrs. Bear.

"I suppose so," said Mr. Pig. "Someone
who knows all the tricks wolves get up
to. Someone who's strong, fast, and scary
enough to scare them off."

"Goodness!" said Mrs. Bear. "It would be the perfect job for somebody who was in earlier today. I'll send him over to you."

Mr. Wolf smiled. Maybe there was hope, after all. When Mr. and Mrs. Pig left, he stepped out of the shadows and slipped back into Mrs. Bear's office.

Mrs. Bear did send him to see Mr. and
Mrs. Pig. Of course, Mr. Wolf had to disguise
himself to get the job. Mr. and Mrs. Pig
would never have hired the Big Bad Wolf.
But a wolf in sheep's clothing? Well, that
was a different matter.

CHAPTER FIVE

Mr. Wolf soon proved just how good he was at his new job too. On his very first day he caught a young wolf trying to climb into the brick house through an open window.

Mr. Wolf pounced swiftly and grabbed the intruder from behind.

"Oh no you don't," he growled in his scariest voice. He sent the terrified young wolf packing.

Mr. Wolf loved his job. He loved playing with the Three Little Pigs and reading them stories.

He had no trouble keeping his paws off
them either. Mrs. Wolf had decided the Wolf
family should be vegetarian. And now they
had plenty of money to buy the food they
needed. The Wolf cubs grew healthy and
happy.

And so, much to his surprise, Mr. Wolf really did live happily ever after!

ABOUT THE AUTHOR

Tony Bradman writes for children of all ages. He is particularly well known for his top-selling Dilly the Dinosaur series. His other titles include the Happily Ever After series, The Orchard Book of Heroes and Villains, and The Orchard Book of Swords, Sorcerers, and Superheroes. Tony lives in South East London.

ABOUT THE ILLUSTRATOR

Sarah Warburton is a rising star in children's books. She is the illustrator of the Rumblewick series, which has been very well received at an international level. The series spans across both picture books and fiction. She has also illustrated nonfiction titles and the Happily Ever After series. She lives in Bristol, England, with her young baby and husband.